When Caterpillars Grow Up

by Lisa Galjanic

Illustrations by Michelle Hope

LSG
PUBLICATIONS

1065 Bay Avenue • East Marion, NY • 11939
29165 Clover Lane • Big Pine Key, FL • 33043

When Caterpillars Grow Up

First printing 2007

International Standard Book Number 978-1-933532-03-5

Library of Congress Control Number: 2005905586

ATTENTION CORPORATIONS, SCHOOLS, PROFESSIONAL AND CHARITABLE ORGANIZATIONS:
Quantity discounts are available on bulk purchases of this book for educational and gift purposes, or as premiums for promoting your organization. For information, contact LSG Publications at www.lsgpublications.com.

For Nicholas and John.
Learn, grow, and delight in life's great adventure.

Special thanks to Allison Antebi, Michelle Cooper, Joanne Hahn, and
Gloria Walko, without whose talents this book could not have been published.

Other titles by Lisa Galjanic

When Leaves Die

When Fish Are Mean

When Squirrels Try

When Bees Win

When Flowers Dance

For ordering information, visit www.lsgpublications.com

When Caterpillars Grow Up

by Lisa Galjanic

Illustrations by Michelle Hope

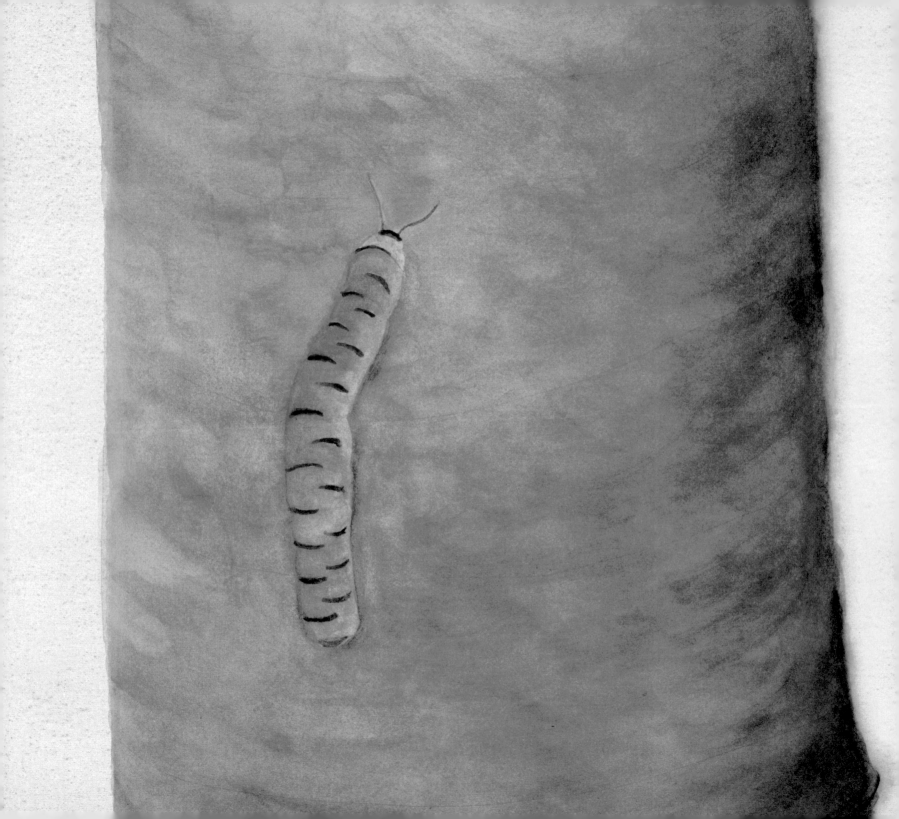

One day, from the bark of a tall tree, a fuzzy little caterpillar set out to see what he could do.

He had many little feet, so he tried walking and climbing.

At first, he
f
 e
   l
     l
and tumbled to the ground.

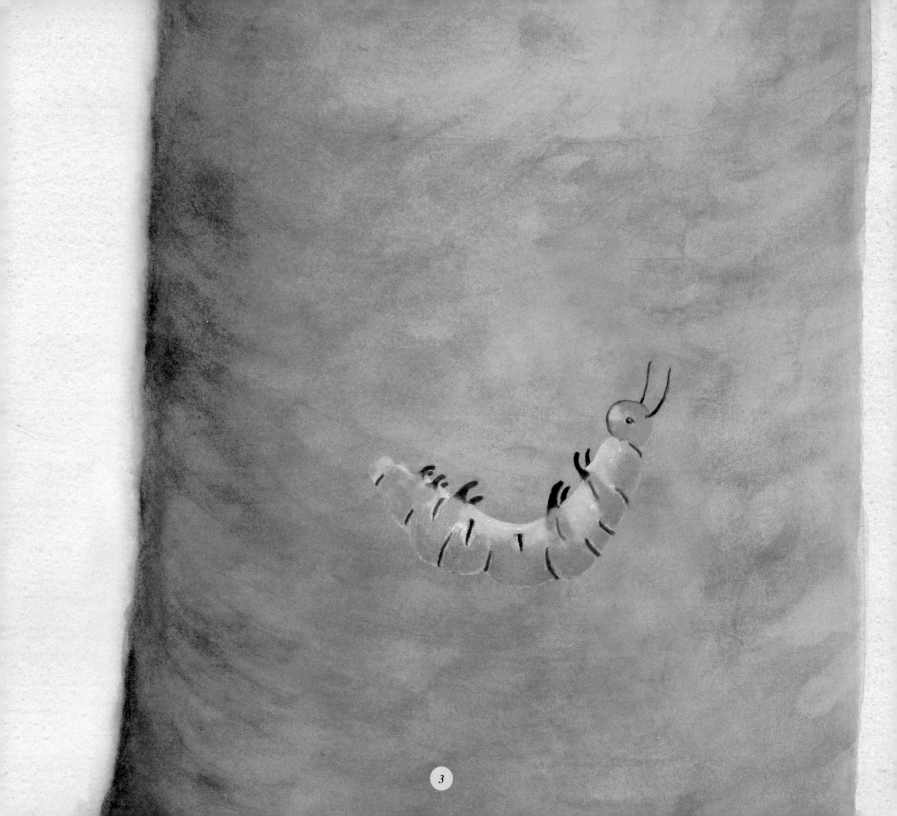

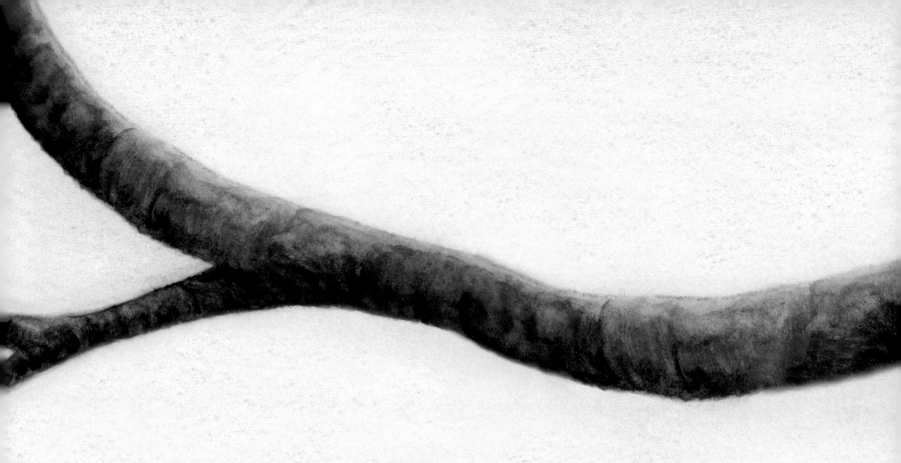

But soon, he became very good at
it. He could even walk and climb
upside down!

He had a very wiggly body, so he tried wiggling this way and that.

At first, he couldn't do much with that.

But soon, he found that he
could stretch very high to
reach the higher leaves that
he nibbled for lunch.

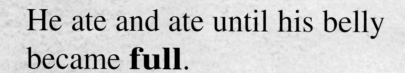

He ate and ate until his belly became **full**.

And he was very proud of himself!

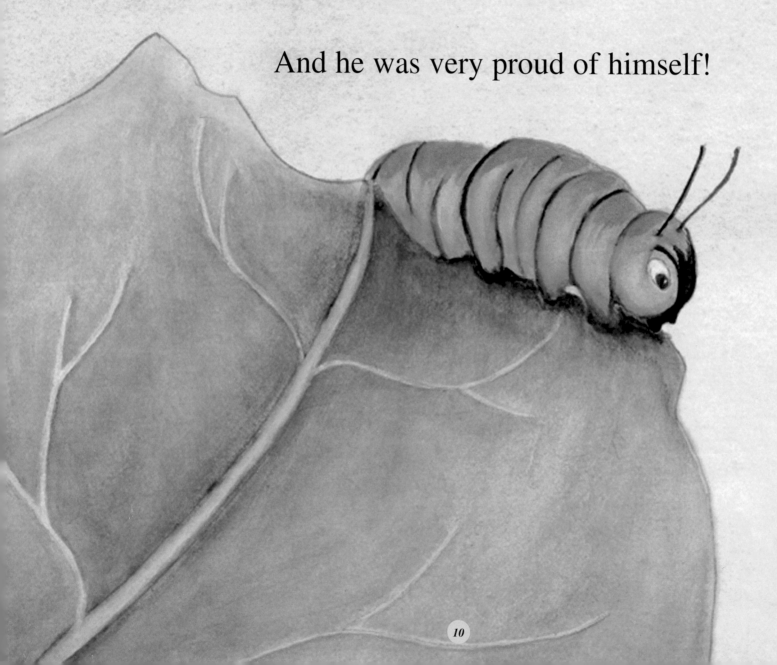

Until …

… one day, after many, many days of
walking and climbing,

wiggling and stretching,

he was bored with the things
he could now do so well.

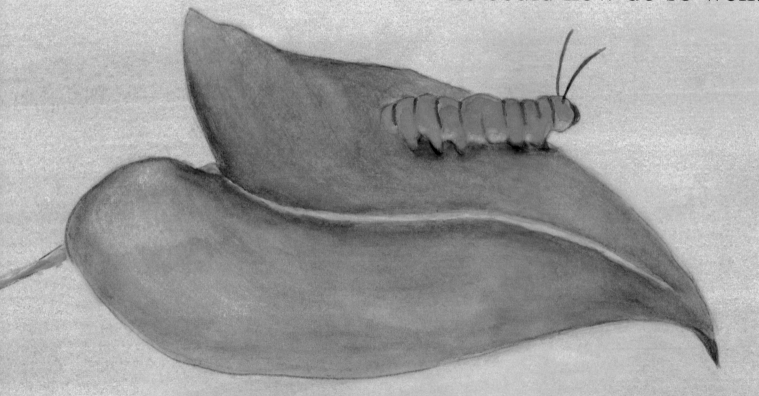

He wanted to do more, but what could he do that he had not already done?

He thought and thought until
he became very sleepy from all
that thinking.

The caterpillar found a soft, warm spot
in the tree where he could sleep.

He made a fluffy white cocoon to
keep him cozy and warm, then wrapped
himself in it and went to sleep.

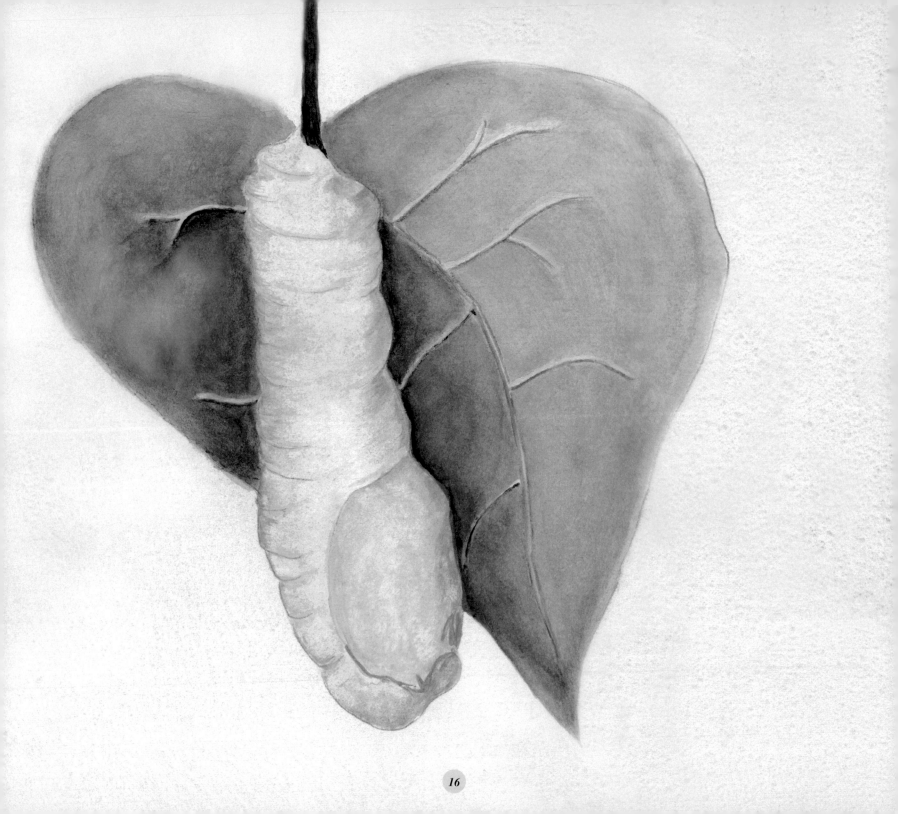

The little caterpillar slept for a
l o n g , l o o o o o n g time.

When he awoke, he popped out
of his white cocoon, blinking
away the sleep from his eyes.

He yaWned
   and stretched
      and wiggled
         and began to walk
            and climb,
               just as before.

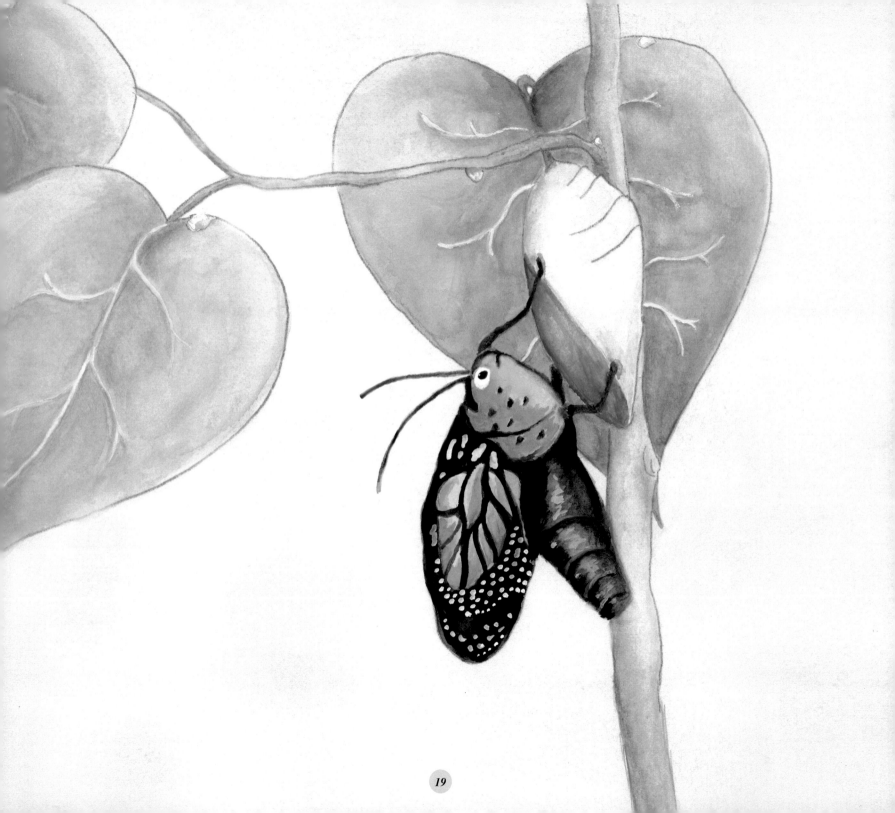

But wait!

As the little caterpillar looked at himself, he saw that he was not a caterpillar anymore.

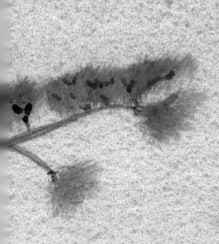

He had grown up to become a beautiful butterfly, with colorful wings that could carry him wherever he wanted to go.

Now, the whole world was waiting for him!

And once again – only now as a
butterfly – he set out to see what
he could do!

Lisa Galjanic, *author*

Lisa is the author of six popular picture books for young children. Dubbed the "When…" series because each book title begins with the word "when," the stories use the antics of familiar animals to inspire children to face everyday troubles with heart, smarts, and spunk. A mother of two, Lisa develops her stories from her experiences in helping her children confront tough situations in positive ways. The "When…" books have been selected for New York's Stories and Soundscapes program, where they are set to original scores and performed by professional actors and musicians for children of all ages. Lisa also dramatizes her works in interactive performances at libraries, schools, and private functions. She can be reached at www.lsgpublications.com.

Michelle Hope, *illustrator*

Michelle is a freelance artist who wants to make a difference. Her philosophy is to "just say yes" to life and live your dreams. Her creative style is simple and unique as she tours the United States on her motorcycle admiring the awe-inspiring natural beauty that is so creatively fulfilling for her. Michelle's motorcycle is her traveling art studio where she uses watercolors to paint nature, her favorite subject. As a mother of four grown children, she believes that children are born with a deep understanding of art and creativity, and she hopes that her illustrations will awaken their inner appreciation and natural ability for art.